Lust Series

Stephanie Dickinson

SPUYTEN DUYVIL
novella series

ACKNOWLEDGEMENTS

Thanks to the editors of the following magazines where hybrids in this manuscript have or will appear: *Hotel Amerika, Skidrow Penthouse, Nano Fiction, Babel Fruit, Blood Lotus, Prick of the Spindle, Oranges & Sardines* (now *Poets & Artists*), *Quiddity, New Collage, South Dakota Review, The Tusculum Review.*

copyright © 2011 Stephanie Dickinson
ISBN 978-1-933132-87-7

Library of Congress Cataloging-in-Publication Data

Dickinson, Stephanie.
Lust series / Stephanie Dickinson.
p. cm.
A novella.
ISBN 978-1-933132-87-7
1. Rape--Fiction. 2. Stream of consciousness fiction. I. Title.
PS3604.I295L87 2011

Lust Series

I wandered from state to state down wild girl sidewalks, sniffing magnolia in full milk-skin bloom. (In humid opening) I wounded my body. I rode scratch marks to this city where the homeless threw themselves (down) on futon cushions, happy to lie in the rain and lunch—midnight apple wine and bread worms. I kissed my lips into garbage cans. I became (one) of them. I rambled from roof to roof sweating starlight and caressing the sleek black rats that gnawed through brick and silt. What did I care about? Wasn't the scar on my face as much truth as any spoke? I stood near the river for the July 4th fandango of sparklers. I chewed the burnt pretzel dough of Christmas. Whiff of reefer, marrow of decomposing Pampers. Then a day as blue as my eyes (came) and a herd of sirens clanged up the avenues, stirring police fire trucks ambulances. As I sat in my kitchen chair on a fire escape I watched buildings die. Blocks away bodies were burning away to soul and in the air voices cried *Tell us how to stay alive.* Billowing black smoke. Enormous (dust). A gaping hole people were falling from.

On a dirt road in their love she feels the deer running through trees. Moon glazes them, dazes grape arbor and pelt. He devours her just as she consumes him. Owls hoot, iced in billion year old light. The dark is a gourmand. It fingers the red maple's coarsely toothed pubis. Licks the sycamore and tulip, swallows the bee winds. On a dirt road far from love pumpkins bloat in the fields between corn shocks, dogwoods gnaw their own hides.

I stood in my lavender nightdress in the wet grass. The man cried before they roped his neck and lifted him off the ground, letting him back down. But still he did not sing out that he killed the girl, so up and down again he went. Proof, they found her stockings on him—pale lilac in moonlight. They cut off the man's toes joint by joint. They started a fire under him with a can of gas. I heard you laugh. Not the you who ate grape pears with me in the orchard. I covered my eyes. A baby shrieked. They hung him higher, quivering with life. You could hear them singing down the street. Fragrance to their singing. Ours simply stank.

When your lust is done with me I'm gonna need a hearse. This fan belt snapping is just another excuse. I'm not a tool. I'm tired and dry. I want to lie down in river water. Your fingers lock the steering wheel, cut off at the knuckles. *Super Bowl Sunday* the motel sign blinks. Dead green neon like scum trapped in pool bottom under the bourbon of stale rain. *There's where we go pay*, I point to a bullet-proof booth like a fast food drive through. A woman in an orange nightgown sits on a stool, her black face white with night cream. You tap the cracked glass, *Ricochet must have done that*. A drawer slides out. Eats our money. Then comes a key looped through a wire hanger. I can feel myself disappearing long before you lift me through the door pink as misery, a black number 9 swinging. All the landscape inside me is shook-up Pepsi. Beaumont refineries, the long tense necks of the naphtha chimneys, the spitty strangling Mississippi. I can't turn back from the pale green asparagus and rain.

All is sex the civet cats going rabid in sweltering ditches, the badger in sloughs disappearing, a screech owl swallowing loose leaves of feathers and flesh, dusty black skin grapes, the boy and the heat lightning he asks to strike her loins. All is sex with the soybeans and ninety degree condensation on lemonade, the tendrils of bloodshot corn silk sweating her cleft, it's the sex of kicked sheets too hot to sleep, pour of stars, blue of the moon on the balcony where a great-great aunt broke her sultry neck beating rugs, not right in the head she jumped a lake of fire and thrush crying out *the black soil is alive*. Ditch lilies fuck orange into the dust. All is sex the wood lily and black-eyed susan, butterfly milkweed and wild rose. Goat's rue gropes the purple prairie clover. Shooting star mounting garlic. Biscuit root and prairie snook. Who plucks out the sun's eye and spits the moon up? Goldenrods quiver in the day's throat, toes dig culvert's honeyed mud and carcass, mellifluous fly wings and mosquitoes. Who makes all this debauch? Crave of tongue and blaze.

Her eye shadow is bruised, a glitter of leopard spots, a coppery sheen he smears over her lids. A cavity in her tooth stabs, her pores are enlarged—birds pecked them; wasps sting her orange lip skin, mouth dry as a saltine. They're having a party in the black sink, more wasps make a comb in her earlobes, the eaves outside stare inside, a window in her forehead admits the smell of refineries, benzene and cymene, and the rapist's name, Larry so plain.

He's bringing in a new girl, making preparations. I watch him as I did the women squatting in the mud to wash their clothes. Heavy as toads they pounded sheets over rocks. My mother beat my father's jeans with her fists. Eyes opened over my face like peacocks fanning their tails, hissing steam in my head. I listened to birds for hours. My mother slapped me trying to wipe the blank stare from my face. Sometimes a single thought tiny as a needle embedded itself in my brain. Stale jewel. I saw my mother's long black hair coarsen. Her wet black eyes dry like paint. I crossed the border. Maybe she carried me. I don't remember. Only Lubys. I bused dishes scraping slop into garbage pails, filled the fat teats of bags, twisted wires around them. Inside more meat than villages ate in a year. At Lubys I fell in love. She worked in the line behind the rolls and breads. Blond hair frazzled her shoulders. Red lips. I couldn't smell cinnamon or eat raisins or flick a pat of butter into the trash without wanting her. So clean. I thought she must be sixteen. I imagined her under my fingers. Velvet skin, moss talk, deer haunches. But she was married with two kids by him. Now he has me cleaning closets, shining the mirror, fixing the dogs on chains out back. He thinks he's strong and can make rivers rise, move the sky like a roof over me. Yet the darkness falls over him too. That first day she brought me here to babysit her kids I read his muscular arms and wide shoulders. He didn't look at me and the children screamed. She loaded a suitcase into her car, and then drove away. She never came back and I stayed. I hunted for her in the closet. Leather jackets and shoes. I stopped counting at 53.

There's plenty of heat even as they walk the cemetery where graves are broken into stumps of salt lick. Tulip and hickory roots snarl and snake over the ground, branches overhead lace together. Nothing has gone into the ground here since 1907. Stones hold down the stillbirths. Scattered, tiny skeletons inside larger ones. Girl-wives bled out in childbirth. Men flanked by bone brides.

I find my way to the bathroom. Everything hurts, my hands, my hazy barefoot eyes blurring in the toilet paper dispenser. I roll the liquid soap between my palms to warm my fingernails, take out my flask of apricot brandy and swallow. There's a radiance wrapped around my head like the glistening of Mary the Sainted Mother or the goddess Marilyn Monroe. Then I realize I am Norma Jean. Armpits sweat dead rabbits. Collarbone broken. I'm dressed in jeans that a shoehorn must have fit me into, red rattlesnake boots, I'm carrying a cattle driver's whip, and I slap the dust from my dark blond hair, shake my head and out come its pins. I take more brandy into me, daub it behind my ears. To know I'm real. Norma Jean looks sad. I tap the mirror, wave and watch bubbles float up. My fingers on the end of galaxies. I pinch a fold of skin above my belly button, all the babies I didn't let live. My first man rises inside me. I was his dancing girl. He talked a three-tier angel food wedding cake. Afterwards I cleaned myself and he joined me in the bathroom. A dark-haired pale man excruciatingly unhandsome. "Don't look at me that way," he said. "What way is that?" "Like you love me." He finished and shook himself. The golden bud of urine on his cock swung. I sat and pulled on my white anklets worn double because my toes shivered, always cold.

Wait for magnolias to close in the stupor of the day. Wait for the swimming pools to take on the faces of morons. You are the blue chlorine hot as French fry grease sunk in the earth and too lazy to raise itself. A street of corn tortillas ready to sex the orange flower milkweed backyard. You are wheat chaff glittering above railroad tracks craving to fuck elevators.

The room smells white, is blue, has pasteboard walls a fist or a feather could pass through into the next welfare apartment, (bare) to blue white striped bed, afghan stuck to the floor in a flame of red ants. Albino cockroaches scuttle, whispery feelers melt into dresser drawers, panties, (silkiness), they wiggle against skin slips. A TV tray is knocked over, corn nuts and cigarette butts scatter. Her lids didn't close and she slept with the whites of her gaze glazed to the ceiling, (floating) on Ativan, into sleep everlasting. A wheelchair smacked against the wall, hair tangled in the spokes, cigarette burns in *On Heroes & Tombs*. Chocolate milk melted Ativan, you must have been high. Heard your body drag across the afghan, hit floor. Imagine (waking) after twenty-four hours, stiffened. Dropping the bridle, a horse races you. Long black tresses already coarse as mane. Indoor Texas. The air conditioner off. 106-degree heat hangs like entrails of flypaper. Eva Braun rigor mortised like this. The SS joked about her pose before barbecuing her beside her Hitler in the Chancellery ditch.

Sun spangles the old branches of a crab apple, a weedy pumpkin grins from the porch rail of a shotgun house. She, the girl who escaped sees cats sunning on the hood of a

chartreuse Cadillac, collapsed on the curb. Three cats— a calico, an orange and a black. "Here, cats," she murmurs, reaching out her hand. The animals are filthy as if they'd just

supped at a grease trap. Their thin fur stiffens, the calico and black hissing before they disappear. The girl half-disappeared herself pets the orange, loosens the goober in its eyes. "I love

you," she says, working her finger under its chin. She feels a long scab like coarse puckered thread. The orange has been in the darkness and fought its way out. She rubs the cat's belly,

touches
stringy
callused
nipples.

Leaves are sweating in her throat. She tries to pull the sun's shadow up to her neck and hide her awkward legs. The soldier speaks and trees become his mouth, his words, hairstreak butterflies. Come out, little one. No, she must stay here in the orchid forest of her body where it is damp and quavering. She pinches her nose to hide the sound of her breath scurrying in and out like wood ants. If the boy-man hears her he will jump, stuff it between her teeth, make her tongue curl into a hyacinth. *Sky Dad*, she whimpers in her mind, *you lied. Nothing about this earth place is what you said.* Not the huge gloom of palmetto shredding like lip skin, the jacuna birds giggling *chitchitchit* from the forest or the fat flirting jacu *splink splinking* in the river as they splash.

Dirty moon. No sky, no Milky Way, all the stars have fallen into the buildings. This isn't the reunion supper with flickering candlelight at a Manhattan bistro, like she fantasized. Although she and her husband are the same age he accuses her of being too old for him. She unwraps the muffin and cuts it into two slabs. The floor under the table is littered with Chinese menus. She picks up *Six Happiness Noodle House*. Slices of white meat simmered in coconut cream and bamboo shoots. Sautéed snow peas with water chestnuts. Boneless duckling served with sweet young ginger root. Like girls being served to aging gourmands.

I'm driving the salvage truck with a septic tank in back. Daddy has his eye on the hitchhiking girls in the pink shirts, the skinny not the fat one. Course with Daddy you never know and that's why I keep my teenage wife beside me at all times, her legs between the stick shift so old Daddy don't start messing where he's got no business. We pick up the girls and it's a tight fit with the skinny one getting the hot seat on Daddy's lap like I predicted. Even with the window cranked down it's sticky and close and grey-chested Daddy keep sucking on that girl's neck, putting hickeys all over the skin he can get to. The old man has the thirst of ten intellectuals and now he's got the vodka bottle, grabbing at the lip, his mouth must taste like burnt cardboard and the place a deer gets brought down and bled out. Maybe the truck is a kind place although there are knives and blood sausage in the glove box and Daddy likes to talk about his gut and maraud days. When and how he made his 19 children. I listen until my ears get a friction burn. That's right 19 of us. I'm the only one honored enough to call him daddy. There's Fort Worth ahead like a stockade of red dust and barbecued ribs, a dry river bed trying to hobble up. The heat is bursting sweat from everyone of us except the girl. Shoot, she's pale as string, all hair flying into his eyes.

Girls drift from buses like fumes while his boots tap the black & white checkerboard tiles between puddles of janitor-in-a-drum. Love's here to fish the girls with red-light district fingernails and ghost town mouths, the women from one syllable Texas cities in purple bedroom slippers. This one drunk on tiredness, this one out of money. Daybreak fires the silver turnstiles of his smile. *Have a match?* Love asks the girl in dirty jeans and butterfly high heels. A scar cuts her cheek, hurts her prettiness. He escorts her across spooky Texas Street's watermelon-colored storefronts. *Where are we going?* she asks, getting inside his ride. Oil and glass towers shimmer--icicles of crushed disco in the unbelievable 102 degrees. *We're going to feel good*, he answers. Desolate subdivisions give up flowering pear and azaleas. Red trees lean like roper's jeans. Underpass girders glitter into salt cedars. She lets Love ride her into the new unbroken day, mockingbirds in peaked hats screaming.

Dog, dog. A small gray animal his neck indented by a collar foams at the mouth. Ditched here in the country so much spittle from his muzzle that it hangs like a lasso the color of churned butter. His fur splinters, each hair a porcupine's spine, his eyes, ponds of blackstrap molasses. The oak shivers and sun whitens the shed roof, slicking the tin until it flows like a river. The rabid dreads water but lusts for it, must have it. His blood is a craving. Oh, want. His capillaries are dry fry pans roiling on cook stoves. Stay behind as he drives himself on toward the shed, forward and back across the pasture. His legs give out, the back two drag. He falls and gets up. It is the water made of tin he desires. *Dog, dog.*

You sit naked on the bank licking pebbles just as the river comes into you, introspective, hot, turning, bobbing you among the slatterns of brocaded weeds. Saw-teeth give way to broad moss plates. Waterlilies, hyacinth's sunken ships, pull you down in their twining, coil your ankles in their past. You glut, bloat into hairbrush stems. Your shoulders strung with bugs, a pork chop of old marrow and lovers. *J'ai gros couer.* The drowned moments take on kisses, cleft chins, high foreheads and cheekbones. A slur and wooziness, the nearness of sex sweet fruit the watersnakes plunder.

Before we met I never liked paralyzed men. The waitress smokes, tries not to meet your eyes. You thump your mug. She stabs out her Ultra Light, scrapes powdered sugar like dandruff from her wrist. The coffee looks embittered the closer it gets. Everything's angry. Sugar shakers with saltine crackers stale and forsaken inside, the maple and strawberry glazed. Drink your coffee. Mine has an injured taste. "Let's take a ride," you say, lifting and stretching your useless legs. To Galveston, to anything, the black leather girls on the seawall sell, their eyes twitchy with white caps and hard-headed catfish. Sling your wheelchair in back. Take your bat from under the driver's seat. Thrill me, hit the accelerator with it. Let's run out of gas in Texas City, coast into a Stop N Go. Pull off your teeshirt. Pass a hand through your hair. It shouldn't be so exciting. The sun is setting as we ride into seawall soaked in a golden glow. We get what we need. Behind us and our well-being, the Gulf of Mexico with shrimp boats floats and tar leaks like a snotty black seaweed. At the Sandpiper motel Quaaludes come on like a thickening dusk. Your skin is impossibly soft and my fingers are lost. In the night you fall out bed and I smile when I hear you cry.

It is cold in this room, the food shivers, coffee growing a skin. I smell the smoked salmon of your shaving lather and ask to kiss your cheek. Lie back, you whisper, promising we'll make love after death. Pushing at my hair with the revolver, you're one long tease. I practice arranging my hands. Night is running out when you press the muzzle against my right temple. In the trees a black blue plumage caws, the unhappy crows want in. I will rise out of my princess gown, the white tulle loops dropping to my feet. I nod, then bite my tongue so I don't cry out. Your little finger's loose nerve twitches like a fishhook. Chastity's silk fan clatters.

A cat was inhaling and exhaling, taking in such long deep breaths the curtains would be sucked from the windows. It must be lying at the foot of the bed. The cat had been in my sleep, a huge Persian Blue sitting in lemon slices and bones of a mullet. I was breathing along with the monster cat. Now it kneaded causing the bed to shift and the sheet to squeak. It made my stomach queasy. I must be on a waterbed. Trying to lift up on one elbow I fell back on the rocking. My head throbbed, headache on both sides of my face, in my jaw. The cat breathing almost made me cry out. Where was I? The last place I remembered being was the white bathroom. Whose room, whose bed? Dirty light seeping in through white curtains. Like lace tablecloths. Breeze billowed the curtains. The movement made me sick. There was a closet with hurricane doors. On my left foot sat the Persian Blue squinting at me with yellow eyes. The cat's fur had grayness to it. The color of hangover. I put my hand over my eyes. My hand burned. I could hardly stand to rest it on the sheet. I shifted my leg and the cat jumped from the bed. Now I could see.

Someone had left rashes on my skin, the red bumps felt like Braille. Who had written messages on my skin only fingers could read? I turned over onto my stomach. I was truly naked. Then I lifted my chin. I wasn't in the bed alone. Next to me lay a stranger. My eyes closed not wanting to know who those shoulders belonged to. I would pick up my clothes and tiptoe into the bathroom. Surely there was one where I could throw up and then find my way to the far away. When I rolled toward the edge of the mattress I noticed a wet spot under me. I shifted but the wet spot remained. A knot formed in the center of my chest. I had wet the bed. I panicked. I buried my face in the pillow. How could I have? I didn't even in childhood. A wave of shame went through me. I had to get out of here without waking the stranger. I stank. The taste of sour and sleep blurred in my mouth. A stickiness on my tongue like drying egg white. Champagne night sweets. I had been down on all fours eating and drinking. Boston scrod, lobster shells, deep dish apple crisp. But how could I get up? I had to cover the wet spot with my body.

A few steps from their desire is a graveyard. Their love doesn't mind the dry breath of a wasp or the scratchiness of a wheelbarrow's handle, the rabbit scuttling through cold brush. They have come here to caress each other, so young not even knowing a car to shelter them. The deer hide here with the human dead, away from the hunters who lure and trap, shooting point-blank at shadows. The boy sniffs the shivering buck, the girl knows the broken brown water of sight trembling in a doe's eyes. Dark blunts the pine needles, blots out the breasts of tawny robins. They lie down to look at each other with their fingers and tongues, to listen to the crackle of corn shocks, beetles purring on the pelts of fungus. The deer listen as they sprint into each other. A greediness to them as they snort.

I'm school dumb. I went to Uncle Bo for hot lunch. Yes, Shrimp etofee and she-crab souffle. Louisiana, we'll go there. Sssssh. Close your eyes. What do you like to eat? Call me Raven. I'm a good bird. I like rice and beans, taste that opens in your mouth. I want to savor you. So Uncle Bo was a flaming fag. He was a fag long before there even was a closet and he flew out of it. Smart fag. He read out big words to me. God is love. I was crazy about him. He wore red satan capes. 'BoBo!' all the kids on the block would scream. He had big muscle arms and little fag hands and would buy us all candy. He told me I was tops. The shango, the yaya chicken. I come from a big family. Nine kids. My mother kept having this and that man's babies. I was second oldest girl. I raised my sisters. I know their bodies about as much as I know my own. I did okay. I'm doing okay. Listen, nobody makes turtle soup out of me. Listen. I'm about love. You ever taste my rice you'll never eat potatoes again. My yams, man. The skins just fall away from the deep sweet. Hear me. Got that. My au sherry, my Commander's Palace Turtle.

County jail girls roll their fingers in ink, admire how their thumbs swirl like underground rivers, their mug shots to be strip searched first. They mount the stairs funneling up, his key fits, a bit rusty but it turns into the half stone light, bleached sun steeped. Cellmates, a mole on her upper lip as if a bird had dropped it there. The other stretches on chains anchoring their bunks, red hair smoky like roasting sweet corn. Mornings, they chomp cornflakes and toast tap water. Lunch, a belch of bologna mustard sandwiches. Then afternoon drags. Snacks are old paperbacks from the 20th. Harold Robbins, the guy's prose so sugary and on the verge of rot, cattle drives and cowboy lovers kneading knuckles to tailbones. The cells across the way hold blind dates, the stickup boys blowing them kisses and tongued lemon drops.

Listen Gulfport, Mississippi, a girl's no washout if she can still buy her liquor not strain three-in-one shoe polish through a powder puff. I've not yet hollered gimme. The sand flies buzz my flask after I take a greasy slurp. Even before I kick past the sign that reads Colored Beach, I whiff it. The stink. Trout that hours ago swam in scoops of spilled cream burn in the bright white sun. A killdeer pecks the hammerhead shark's eye. Second sight. I can see my future ending with this day's light. Not on this beach but outside the city limits I'm going to hemorrhage in a car wreck. Lover man, should I try to escape, try floating out into the tide? What lingerie these Portuguese men-of-war make, fringed moon jelly and sequined fish scale.

The torn cotton of her panties are shackled men dragging gunnysacks, boll weevils, thorn and itch, scratch of seed hairs and lint-cut fingers. You crawl through her things out of boredom. A gold-painted cherub throws dim 40-watt suns on stretched elastic and crotches of shredding cocoon. Briefs washed by lye have gotten her through a long widowhood. Surprised by a layer swaddled in wax paper your fingers wade to drawer's bottom—cream-colored panties cut below naval with rosebuds seep a rich lilac stink. Trying them on you touch sweltering summer—the last time these panties wore flesh. *Oh god.* Slipped shivering to ankles these lush entrances knew what it was to be wanted. Suckling covetous moths.

She sees the door that he's locked from the outside, knows the spare room of love is customized. His feet in flipflops are drifting across the living room. He's removing his brown moleskin pants. The spare room takes quick little breaths, no chance she'll escape. In the windows there are flies laying eggs. She's alone with the cardboard boxes. Her hands burn from his textbooks. She sleeps, startles to him dressed in a hooded Jacob's robe. He pushes her into geology: Tectonic plates, continental drift. Asteroids, the five thousand year old tidal wave. Lake Sam Houston spills mutated catfish onto its cement banks. A red snapper cries out. Lilac-eyed fish wash up. A boy is shot three times and winks from his coffin satin at a woman and is shot twice more. An amberjack slain, awakens. Flayed. Pines alive with maggoty shadows whiten sheetrock walls. Forests. More flames. The flies go silent. After days he takes her into the bathroom to wash her in the black sink and sit her on the only obsidian toilet she's ever seen. Its lid is swaddled in blood-plush fur and the tissue dispenser too wears a red pelt. A rack of lightbulbs licking water from the faucet. In the black tub a rubber duck spreads webby feet and clatters from yolky beak. Wiped clean of love, he leads her into the living room and unbolts the front door, pointing. Past sweating filth magnolias and petal lampshades, into spike of yuccas fanning their blades, through odors of blue cheese and dog turds. Don't look back. That is the way, away. The kitchen cupboards with their flat plastic roach traps hiding behind counters send out flirtatious giggles.

Hemmed in by mewling pumpkins, stick-pelts of bouquets, the car vanishes into half-light. You squat in the orchard of stones & shards, nose your hand into the rusted earth, imagine digging down toward a pale moon of a bone in drawstrings & ecru lace. Your lover looks on. You both need something that has been lying in darkness a long time as if deer eating the dusk isn't enough. Overhead the black & blue plumage caws, the disgruntled crows want you out. Better to be a bobcat stalking, mouth-eyed, who stared with teeth at the first diggers, shoveling & scratching to store up their beloveds, before leaping.

If this is for old times sake you pleading with me to record again I don't need it and although I've had to mend my pearls and silk back button drawers, I have enough to drink (corn brew) and take no guff from anyone. When the bills come round I put myself right before a gin house crowd and rattle their teeth—six feet and 200 lbs.--Baby Won't You Please Come Home in a shimmy of ostrich plumes that had the luck to meet that special someone who doesn't need chasing with a gun. Like that sweet ex-daddy who went skirt sniffing a chorus girl with skin no darker than the bruised flesh of a yellow moon and last I saw he was slurping crawfish and Tabasco sauce, his eyes aglitter like diamond stickpins he'd dig out if he'd thought they'd hock.

I hear Whaylen's breath take a deep exhale and I twist his hair around my finger. It squeaks. "You go on to Fargo, Whaylen, maybe that will put Betty straight." My voice even to my own ears sounds blurred and dry. New snow flurries. Shoot, Whaylen's always afraid Dixie, his thirteen year old, is going to run away with a good for nothing and sleep under bridges, afraid his ex-wife Betty is drunk and in back of cars with high school guys. *My favorite was Elizabeth, my youngest, my sweetest, my Downs Syndrome. It was her death that finished me. That's her on the dresser in the royal blue velvet dress. Have you ever seen lips so red? Cherries just pitted. It's Saturday and the afternoon programs are on. Tonight, I'll lie with the high school boys. They have lips that hurt to kiss. The juice from them bleeds on the tip of your tongue and I'll think of her blond hair. Color of the Yellow Medicine River.*

Leaves parachute into my mouth that squirrels eat so I no longer know if what they gather is some remnant of my flesh. I taste of haunting strong aroma, yellowish-white July peonies, of clay. In my ear hollow bones and wind, a tongue of rope skin and bark split from a tree. I want to be flung into words and sentences, songs made with soft tissue of throat, all the left behind weedy horse chestnuts, buckeyes with shine like irises of mares, the red mulberry, what the green asks.

Desire and appetite on the sidewalk. Barrels of sea onions bob like poached eyeballs. Squids lie in ropy tentacles against groupers and blue fish. Salted cod in crumbs of snow. Stew fishes of fragile driftwood. The fish are beautiful. She wants to kiss them. Men lean into crevasses. They look. A man pushes his shopping cart piled high with empty milk gallons. He hisses. She gazes at shop windows. The Pork Chop. The suckling pig. She smiles at the fatty corpuscles and muscles that rim the eyes. Even the snout is shaved. A heap of pigs feet draws her eyes. Enormous cloven hooves white except where blood has settled leaving them red blue and bruised. A washtub of what looked like hide with hair fibers bristling from it. Who craves this? She yearns to walk through the window, freeing her skin from muscle on shards of glass. Then the tallow animals will quiver, making room for her to sit.

Dawn breaks on Lake Street, the suicide of moon on the block of wrecked Minneapolis mansions. Ice congeals the cast iron of street. Fifty miles south, trapped into five-month winter, her hometown Redwing grovels under snow, barns and farmhouses stagger, mastodons, streaming filthy fleece. Enough for a week's rent the chasm in their ceiling makes space for another room to fit between her and the chandelier of flame-shaped blackened bulbs. He grips his red wine. His breath is sticky-sweet-blood from a sucked cut. "*It's finished, I tell you*," he bites a thread on the sleeve of his tuxedo. "*I want to practice the silence.*" Black hair hangs to his waist. Different from the sons of Swedes she grew up with, their blond hair the color of desks. She loves him. His scorching yeastiness. His hands encircle her burgundy sheath, hem of boa feathers. Her eyes are chunks of blue ice. Her mouth a smear. A Chinese princess brought to the Forbidden City with a half-eaten kiss on her lips. "*Get out of here*," he whispers in her ear, "*unless you're coming with me.*" His ancient Underwood shudders—its ribbon pulled from the spool, keys gummed together. He's burned almost everything. His unfinished manuscripts, *Mon Hysterie, Chorale,* --

the reams of famished weeds and belly dancers.

Wading through the soft sea with an eye of iron.

One fragment. Like reading Revelation on the first day of a decade. He's a genius, she thinks. The next Rimbaud. His excess fills her larynx, loosens her heartbeat. If he wants her bones, she'll gladly give him those.

"*Art for art's sake.*"

We undress each other under the piano and I get the pedals up in my hair. The upstairs is a below zero and even the mattress shouldn't spend the night with only one sheet. We pile coats on and I kiss him goodnight. "You're not as good looking as father," I tell him. "So? You're not as pretty as mother." That's a lie. I'm wavy black hair to my waist, blue eyes and church steeple cheekbones. We fall asleep wrapped around each other and maybe we'll wake with the sheet iced to our skin or better yet to not wake and our last touch frozen solid my fingers to his lips. I'd rather breathe in snow, his leg thrown over me, crushing me with his night breath and then wanting me like that. The starlings gather on the barbed wire fences, their winter eyes bright red, yellow freckles in their feathers. I have nicks in my flesh from their beaks. Trees are roaming around. I won't look at them, but they're running toward the house, wailing Bonnie, Bonnie. Struck by moonlight the birches are begging for someone to cut them loose too. They watch with widened black eyes the damnation of my brother and I.

Every warm and cold-blooded being has one—the luminescent
blue Carpathian Scorpion,
the Yellow-Headed Scolio,
    the Short-Toed Eagle,
    the Long-Legged Buzzard,
    the Red-Rumped Swallow,
the Lesser Spotted Eagle,
the Ground Squirrel,
the Marbled Polecat,
    the Cotton Rat,
    the Grasshopper Mouse.

Suddenly the trustee opened the cell and led you down stairs past the accused rapist, through the murky bare bulb into the jail's corral. Lips painted white, you thrilled—a visitor to witness you. Nineteen, patchouli-drenched, copper bangles, twenty on each arm, you had metamorphosed into someone. You saw your mother rise, leave her purse on the graffiti-stained table, her arms that smelled of brown sack and celery dying at her sides. Who is that with the bare stomach? Jeans dragging, you pranced to her, batting your ghoulish lashes. "What have you done with my daughter?" she whispered. Fifty-nine that day, her big hands smoothed her injured dress. Great Mother Cybele raised by panthers, her love too intense for her mortal. Your goddess is a short shy woman with badly dyed hair. Pocket gopher.

Wolves,
jackals,
all kinds of Ungulates.

Pilot of a Liberator B-24 missing in action over Sicily since July 4th 1943. How beautiful he is in uniform, the mustache and long lashes, peering out from this yellow newspaper column. Son of the cornfields and Carrie Worley, ("Dig dig," she said to her other son, "go to Sicily and dig until you find your brother.") Not dirt but shot from sky into Mediterranean azure his body and the photo he took with him. Two bathing suited girls, the prettier one's stare meets his, in her eyes there's sultry stephanotis on the wilt. He was the best dancer, this plankton pelted skull who loves the brazen one. *My heart belongs to you.* Bones leeched to a dying coral reef. The plain girl stares into the sun. *I'm yours.* A sizzling minuet meets hatchet
fish.

The first time love felt like coming back to life it was spring after a hard blizzard. Love had been maimed, rocking herself in a closet to somehow bring back the girl who was. Halved raw, wet feathers again lopped in brine and currant jelly, a second birth, as if waiting for teeth to break from her gums, as if sounds not yet become words or thought scoured from a bramble of sentences. From all fours love climbed back to two feet. Enrolled at a prairie college stretching to the Dakotas Wounded Knee Blue Lake New Ulm Redwood Falls. The brick had barely lifted its lips from the teats, new among ramshackle farmhouses that stood down long breathing lanes. Here the ruddy skin of red stoned dormitories, science buildings domed with smoke plexiglass like flying saucers piloted by androids, a freakish examining by moonlight of the snow with its throat cut. Nothing in those bodies and buildings could teach love how to live. Like farm boys around girls who shuffled their feet, although they'd helped birth piglets and seen afterbirth flower from the humid womb of sows. Sky mounted the plains, an ink-blue wilderness of barbed wire trying to pluck its thorns from the wind. Eighteen, her arm in a sling, metal fused to bone, none of it mattering to love who was coming back into this girl. She glowed with a beautiful wounded sheen. Hair straight to her waist, frail in a blue cape, a brokenness trying to pretend that love was is could yet be again.

Down here in the orchard of mud, I find a face, eyes like buckeyes. Is it the pony I lost so long ago? His muzzle is velvet mire, his mane, chestnut sediment. I am trying to gather my mud next to his flank. What could I trade to have my hand for an instant? To raise a wave. My hair the birds took to nest in the yellow locust. The red mulberry has uses for me.

You are the time beside the mailbox flag when ditch begins to creep from its shoulder and slides into the corrugated pipe--degrees stagnant under the quilt of the road. You are plain and foursquare. You are the dinner bell ringing, thudding past oak trees, the sweaty cattails afloat in civet bones. You, dense as midday dinner the threshers devoured sixty years ago in Black Hawk County. You command the locust to drone, man calling woman to the dirt nest. Singing to the girl who lies in her girl grave, you eye shadow her, bruise her, make her a glitter of green cow spot, a coppery sheen. You smear her over with your elaborate erection, purple folds. You are that tar brush and claw opening her neck, for blood to flow from her mouth to her feet, jaguar with penis, jaws licky red with liver and heart, the bread meats eaten. You offer her to the gravely sky.

Kept here on Mustang Island in the Sheridan, her lover allows her to leave the room and ride the elevator with him to Sunday brunch. She watches the black slug of an oil barge sit on the horizon as people crowd in, the women and men here to fill their bellies are brightly dressed. With too many pairs of arms and legs, their tongues slip back and forth. Today he forces her to feast. She is fingering the slices of ham carved from the hock, licking cantaloupe balls. Honeydew and pineapple wedges spill from a gutted watermelon. Paradise's best kept secret. She wishes she were down on her hands nosing the starvation grasses. He forces her to swallow more chocolate crepe. Once this belonged to the Karankawa. Wild women were kept with horses. Men captured other men. On ritual days virgin girls ate the long meat, broke human bones and scraped the marrow. "What an animal you are," he remarks, his fork edging onto her eggs benedict. It was forbidden to cut the sexes or remove the bladder so urine could not poison the white meat.

Nut berries hang from barren branches. Farther up the trees are fruited with petrified oranges. They attract her although the fruit is dead, a dying so dry so different from the riverbank's sour. Teeming. She picks an orange, holds it to her nose, dehydrated. It has the odor of sex, milk-fleshy, slit. She puts it to his nostrils. Offers him their odor, love on a mattress, between rocks, what can't be washed. He tells her he knows where skin comes from. Easy, the sap that dries between her thighs. Minnows whirl, leech up the hill, stones break tumbling from earth socket to murder all the particles of follicle and tendon trying to carry his slouch into her womb.

The first honky tonk I sang Rent House Blues to stomped and threw peanut husks after I draped a boa of chicken feathers from my shoulders while Rabbit Foot Minstrels riffed stride piano. I was a girl the color of meat smoke on stage with grease painted Ma Rainey, who never said create new melodies like me, but swaggered this street busker into limousines and Detroit buffet dates. Ma in her gold-dollar necklaces licking over to say she's crooked and soon she'll introduce me to plenty high yellow girls who don't like men. I poured down tumblers of gin while Ma strung her five and ten and twenty pieces to her neck in her whisper louder than a field holler.

She hungers like a mushroomer. Her breasts wear orange straw hats & carry tiny paring knives. All night she tramps the maroon puddles & brackish leaves--the dark places where they dwell—pale mushrooms, musky toadstools—grayish-purple fungus. She gropes the shapes that are edible. She finds pieces of dark pink moth orchid to stuff in her mouth. Sweet, redeemed earth where love is. She reaches the bank where hardwoods greet her, the moon shining wishy-washy on the fungus creeping up trunks. Everywhere the pastel flesh is crumbling from fallen logs. Then the hunger changes. Like a predator she scents the gobbets of blood sweetening the salt water. Sailors swim toward her jaws, her pelvic fins tipped with black, her gigantic grey-bronze body. She takes transoceanic trips of ecstatic biting & digesting. Still the prey come to her triangular teeth haunted by baby elephant seals. Her snout parts & in crowds the oarfish, jack, barracuda, tuna & squid. Ballerina slippers of vomited silk.

"Where did you learn to kiss?" he asks. Did she really live in Texas, Oregon, Louisiana—all the states she claims? How many lovers? A streak of sweat salts his temple and leaks down, hangs from his earlobe like a sweet pearl onion. Her tongue strains as hairs on his back rise like iron filings. They met for the first time since high school tonight. Another drop of sweat streaks his cheek. The joint he lights reminds her of the ham served at the banquet. With gray curling edges the ham gave off an incredible sadness. She wanted to pick up a cut and kiss it. Against her leg, his sex hard as ear corn. She wonders if they're tempting fate. There is the screech of a faraway train. Their classmates, sixteen year old Mary and Chris, flicker in the candle light. They have come back from their crash to watch the couple on the bed rut. The two who missed their lives.

Big-knuckled, my boy fingers kneaded cow udders until I educated them into chemists. I took them to California, discovered a eucalyptus woman and wedded. (*dear purpling hibiscus your ashes are scattered in the Pacific.*) Each year more of me disappears. I haven't heard *Francis* said aloud in years. No striped mullet, roof rat or human has called out *Francis. Francis, come out. Whatever you are.* I am the tyrant who said when and if light in my children's rooms went on. Weak as frogs my offspring, the boy ate clay, the girl drove into a guardrail. Black night herons eat their own young, swallowing the head first. The white ibis devours its own eggs. Here clouds the color of dirt settle over my face. I want to stop earth turning against the blade. To silence the hooves of horses, their bones jutting at my elbow, to shut up leghorns cursing the red fox against my jaw. Open my mouth against the forenoon sun, I did not know the horse chestnut tree would grow through me or what forms I'd become. Flesh skin hair mud and twig.

I found you on the internet. Creamy petals, you named me. Haunting powerful surrealism. We met up close and I skipped rope each swing, a lash as it hit the floor and you sat at your keyboard, the poem was on its way. 50 times I jumped with my right foot 30 with my left. You were hammering it out. Later I worked your flesh dough. You ate my nipples. I rested my head on your glutinous stomach. *Patty Cake Baker Man.* I thought you would breathe sonnets into me. You were just a man's tongue, a pulp I sucked coffee and menthol from. When I surprised you with cookies I found another chat room student. I could shoot you, shoot you both in the neck so you'd bleed better. Dante, Poor Tom the blabbering idiot in Will Shakespeare's Lear, John Donne, all of them nothing but window dressing. I'm pulling down the shelves, scattering manuscripts. Me, psychotic? Who do you think you are? My father's gold card?

Tease, he smiled. His hands trembled when he clutched her shoulders. His nose began to run and he pulled a handkerchief from his pocket. I knew from first minute that you'd been got to early, he said. She'd never before seen a handkerchief in real life. When the interview ended she went to the refrigerator and picked from the lunch meat pack a slice of spiced ham. Poor people food, he pointed out. His housekeeper's. He liked to watch girls eat. She spooned mayo straight from the jar into her mouth. But she wasn't at all hungry and that frightened her. She hated to leave the avocado appliance. Air hung religiously around the ice maker. He pinched her bottom and elsewhere. Goodness what a morsel you are. The asinine bubbliness was in her head along with foam from the corner of the old accountant's mouth, taste of cooked asparagus, which she disliked. She moved lazily over piled carpets ignoring gilded frames flashing gold at her from table tops. He escorted her into his study, then went out to change from his suit into a bathrobe. He showed her his left mannequin leg that he lifted gingerly onto the desktop. It did not match the pale right one threaded with occasional hair. He'd been run over in his driveway by his ex-wife. "Instead of braking, she hit the gas. I don't believe it and neither do my lawyers." Her eyes were riveted to the leg that wore a shoe, really quite masterful. She would sleep in that remarkable woman's bed. The day what she could see of it through purple drapes and Venetian blinds seemed perfectly still, an adverb day.

Where is the bat of the cave, the frog, the honey-bee north eastern? All is blind, ur-magnetized, pew-hush & cavern-emptiness. Red-eyed in clammy cold home, no brood, no webbed wings & mammalian babies in fur nap and milk. Blooded cousins of the dark who white mildew kills. Here legs fishnetted & stiletto, here 1:30 am on parade. Where enchantment? Where water lily? See-through girls march scented lilac & musky-rose—diamond drop earrings on sullen grey jowls of night. Gold over gold bought & sold. Great dying is everywhere. We step through puddles of piss, call it
perfume.

Rimrock. Why he picks me up at high noon off the highway and takes me deeper into the swirling dust—the red clay flagging down the speed limit, is anyone's guess. The clouds blow smoke rings into gashes, wind devils, and on the horizon—cliffs, knobs rock. He's been driving decades down to windpipe and hip bones.

Hear the fright that happened here eons ago. Hear teiid lizards scrape their tails through the bald petrified cypress and fossil fern. He served in Korea. Ate dog stew. About to turn himself into the VA for treatment. Veterans of every war roam these desolate places, known by the wild spaces in their eyes, presentiment like his waking hours where prehistoric gar frolic shale oceans of fern rot, lizards that taste through their skin. An ice age later I stick out my thumb beside a road sign. He tells me only electric shock can wipe out the dog stew and Seoul cold.

The bulleted girls.

Once the black at the back of my closet frightened. Now I was buckskin boots and a lipstick smear in hundreds of miles of rimrock. A pony print dress. Nineteen, mad to travel into gashes and gut, scout the intestine of butte. I thought I was about to be murdered and wrote my name on match books, proud that splinters of my cheekbones would someday be nosed up by prairie gophers. I wish I'd disappeared with him into the unfinished interstate.

Death. It's supposed to be a bright white light instead there's a girl shouting, her pouty mouth a spoiled gardenia, who likes walking in the dark to the sound of the creek, her black hair roosters have scratched in every direction.

Drifting in overcast, water and sky where men sit all day and fish. Cranes perch in the mist that goes on and on. It's still except for the mullets that blurt from the water like they're being shocked, without scale, rouged creamy skin like the high inside of a girl's thigh. Mullets. Men. Flat heads, eyes oil-black, disturbing, pre-Christian. The men are using minnows to fish with. How many eons to make one? They're living in the pail, silver ringlets, and some blue, some pink, will-o-wisps. Men bait their lines and cast. The minnow swims away from the boat with the hook. It has to be alive for the fish to bite. Sun has fallen into the bayou and mullets jump, flying from the water, ten, twenty feet, trembling with the murk of the underwater.

You flick the switch. I jump; I swallow the hook deep.

I crossed the field sometimes so I could buy purple bubble gum and I'd keep it behind my bed-board where the little horse was carved into the wood. I'd chew and then stick it onto his left ear and the horse didn't mind because I'd find gum there no matter how many days later. I liked sunflower seeds and pop tarts and Ferris who lived across the road and whose barn I could see from my window would bring them to me. When he'd cross the field walking into Ely, I'd follow. Mom worked in town and Pa was a hired man. I'd meet him where the grain elevator bloated with Kent Feed sacks, the shuck of grain, fragrant hot with ground corn cobs burning the air. Ely I could smell the hatched chicks in heat, lick the yellow of their feathers.

Louise left the door open and I walk into her legs sprawled over the couch. Crap she feeds herself and her kids, cornflakes, koolaid, poptarts, making even her toes fat.

"You got my cigarettes?" she mumbles.

"Yeah, I got your cigarettes. Wipe the sleep from your eyes, mama, your man's got something for you. Didn't get dressed today, did ya?" Before she answers I let my wet jeans drop and slide the blanket she's been cuddling with up over her head. She ain't Louise anymore, who has seen better days, her bleached hair the color of overeasy eggs. I just want to cuddle with her, just take the warmth from her body. She could be Jackie Mae, the girl who came from down south in the seventh grade with her big knockers she more or less hid in overalls and her long hair mostly wind-whipped and never washed too often. Her father, a hired man, moved them into the farm house across the road. I was crazy about her southern accent, her sad brown eyes outlined with black junk, even her acne—the kind that goes layers deep. Girls said she stunk, but I loved her.

Inside a Japanese music box she scented clay odor, then tasted the night's sleep in your mouth as you mounted her. "Maintenance," you grunted. She laughed and closed her eyes, seeing the red-eyed Kabuki actors applying wax to their eyebrows and white face cream on their cheeks, princess and commoner practicing samurai sex. You in goldenrod panties. You singing the muffled traffic of the streets below. You saying, "Hey," into her ear, "I'm going to taste you." You, between her legs, your breath tickling the inside of her thighs, your blond hair meeting her darker hair. You trying hard to please her, and her shame of where your tongue was/is, her quivers growing stems, musky and filled with French sauce, you gripping her knees, ordering her to become a puddle of muddiness an orchid shudders from. But she didn't let it out, would go only so far toward the edge even with you, she couldn't dissolve. In the heaven of predators, she never let her guard down, and practiced leaving her body, swimming with the flatfish, the skates and ray swordfish, the triggers and puffers, all prey.

Was he trying to cut the blood off to his testicles? How ugly testicles were. May apples in pimpled red skin. Reject baptism, exorcism. He lifted my legs, bending them back; putting me in position for a somersault. A relic of the Roman Catholic. He wasn't going to do this to me. I wasn't going to let him. Shame filled me. I was dirt and it didn't matter what you did to dirt. I wasn't dirt. I was as good as anyone, better.

I would enter a temporary agency, register, take the written filing, spelling, capitalization, and grammar tests, scoring one hundreds, and then it would be time to take the dreaded typing test on a IBM Selectric. There would be a page from an old secretarial school manual on the typing stand with tongue-twisting phrases like *future minimum annual gross rents to be received on noncancellable leases* or *The Institute ("Institute") founded in 1894 as the Society of Beaux-Arts Architects*. An egg timer would be set. Three minutes of terror. 70 wpm under pressure *Beaux-Arts Architects*. I must have really been a looker then. Now frosted blond hair, though I still soldier on wearing it in a ponytail. The same forehead and cheekbones as Jamie, definitely his height, but while his body is broad and blunt, mine is one of those wrap-around vamp bodies that can snake over furniture, coil and uncoil, making sure it draws everyone's eyes. My generation of women haven't miscalculated what power is, only think their way of getting it is through men. Jamie says I used to set an egg timer while he ate. He claims he had to eat so fast that he threw up. I made him eat his puke. Don't believe it. The sacraments have no magical power.

Dear Free World Lady

I think of you until my mind gets tired. Your mouth and eyes. My petite, five-foot, ninety-two pound Cajun Angel. I'm not going to lose you, just hang on to your blood cells until I'm out. Twiglet, when you see your old man again, you'll figure he's Mr. Atlas. I've been devoting myself to squats, crunches, leg raises, followed by six-pack power minutes. Remember the old days when we'd snort cocaine in Seven Eleven bathrooms enjoying a little vacation from the everyday self? We both loved the bitter as it dripped down the back of our throats. The lost feeling of the white powder inside us, a bird of loneliness, piggy perches with checkerboards of faded blue. I'm taking a writing class. Teacher thinks I've got talent. Lots of the guys here would do anything for a female pen pal, someone from the Free World to correspond with. Especially the Death Row dudes locked down in 6x9 cells 23 hours a day.

After the stickup, you promised we weren't hiding out in any no-tell motel, we'd pitch a tent back from the road that clutched the lake and the 100 degree suck of a five month heat wave. You and me were going to roll around in the white mushroom glow plucked from the moon and listen for the green-hooded armadillo thwacking in the brush, nosing with his long snout. Liar, it was a $42 dollar a night room you brought me to, empty but for the a/c turned up to ice. "You're a beautiful man. I love you," I said, kissing your collarbone. You belched, "Goddamnit there's a cockroach on my shoulder." After that I didn't think I could eat a French fry without ever crying.

Dear Free World Lady

Another day in the broomcorn. Picture six foot brooms stuck in the ground with pointy gray-green ears. It's evil to look at. (Do they sell this stuff or is it just special convict crop to torture us with?) A flatbed moves forty men into the distance of those little hills. The Looker rides his dirty mare. He's got a scope rifle. More mounted bosses slinging shotguns count us off into hoe squads. Rubberneck starts at his end, I start at the opposite, and we weed until we meet in the middle of the all-day row. I keep pulling weeds that don't come out of the ground easy, 'cause they have roots like trees. Have to use your bare hands to get a grip, and don't forget a sprinkle of lye pesticide. We're good at killing. A chicken hawk circles, waiting. I'm sweating and about to fall out. I think of you and not the girls at Caligula's in yellow silk teddies—the ones you'd always accuse me of wanting. I'd look into their lids of mercury, half-closed, reminding me of things with poked-out eyes. I'd deliver them their angel dust and watch their faces do a rise like in thermometers. I never touched one of them, never had the desire. I made mistakes wanting to be a player. I didn't want to sit on the bench or play second string. Now I'm sidelined. I'm sorry, lady. You could have done better. What I wouldn't give to have a cat in here.

Moon passes under a bread wrapper cloud and goes out. Bowery graveyard. The dawn is a window grate fire escape, a blurred curtain. Dawn noses the pale stones sunk into dirt. What once was cow lane now skyscraper-siren and a derelict's whiff of rotting peach breath. Here the fleshed undead sleep bundled in pages of flophouse Gideon Bibles, here the living are filled with thirst that gnaws at their bowels. Wind shakes the hackberry, furrowed green dryads wedding Hudson to East River. No sky here, only blinking satellites and mica-flecked twin phantoms. Sweetish smell of burning hair.

Prairie Moon sticks in your head, the joint you used to sneak to, the forbidden dancehall with its chip of blue neon moon burnt into ice-homicide parking lot. A live band yodeled from the stage as you strutted in lipstick and black fishnets, your hand Day-Glo tattooed PAID. In a booth gouged with initials, his cheek reeked of *Schlitz*. He dared you to drink the tin pop-top and because you were fourteen and he, a big sixteen sacker at the Jack & Jill, rough X's on his nails from slicing them with boxcutters, you put it in your mouth. He stopped you, his personal hick, who wore *Tabu* perfume under her armpits. Was it love with the sacker because he sweated so much? His fingers snagged your stocking legs. He ground his cigarette out in your hand. To be beautiful, a thing needed to be ruined. You figure it's the neon that makes even the wound blue. Like someone waiting to be taken against the chain link fence festooned with razor wire.

I keep running the hurt in my side running too until the ground pulls me down and I taste the bitter twigs. The shatter of his laughter. *Your deer is dead.* He cuts me around each knee. My leaping, hoof stampedes. He tugs my skin and flesh. Slashes my windpipe. I make no more groan or sing. From my belly no more fawn. My guts try to get away. Behind me the trees stand beginning to vanish. I call for the sky to come back. He wipes his knife on the same grass he found poking in my stomach. Bitter dandelion and shad grass. He unfleshes my bones and says he is dressing me.

The red candle is in your hand. You light the taper. I watch the drops of wax fall onto my back. Hot seed, tears of blood. Flickering banshees, cross-eyed devil men, Japanese samurai. Hot wax doesn't feel like much, it itches, a flicker and then nothing. There's something about pain, even a tiny cut or a bruise, that soothes. "How does that feel? Feel good?" I think of the 72 eunuchs to be found in the list of Christian Saints, which indicates the special place castration has earned in Christianity. Italy where until the end of the 18th century, 4,000 boys were castrated a year to supply the church choirs. I hear them sing. In Mother Russia. I see the flagellants in the birch forests whipping themselves. This is what it is like to live in a world where belief is everywhere and God, the evening wolf, so close at hand you smell his yellow breath. I want that. I want to be someone the inquisition is looking for. Anyone, even some small-fry friar who has written a tract in the vulgar tongue. Instead I see your shoulder, the large freckle.

Even walking two steps behind you there is still so much sidewalk and many eyes. Blue peacocks. "Don't look at the stores," you say. "They have cameras." The video can capture what I see—the murdered girl riding between your shoulder blades, your thumbprints in her neck. Her white skirt and silver belt. Her red tears. Cold. That's why you're wearing sweatpants in ninety degrees. You're ice. Because she is. You keep cracking your knuckles, the fig cookies smack, your tongue paddle mashing seeds and saliva. Since we left New Jersey you can't seem to stop eating. Fruits, nuts, slugs. A dim sky hangs starless between buildings. Ticker tape Times Square. BODY OF MISSING NEW JERSEY GIRL FOUND IN DUMPSTER. News chases the lit up letters into the blank. Legs fishnetted, see-through girls walk by in bursts of perfume. Lilac. Rose. Diamond nose studs in the gray face of the night. You stink like homicide.

"Wait!" I call out. "I need to go in here." Before you can stop me I dart into Designer Perfumes. Rustling manes of fragrances rush at me. The stronger ones, the weaker. Others wait for me to go toward them. I smell like grilling sweat, like soy sauce and Clorox. Like a bird at the base of its quills. I smell like a dead girl. Not blood. There wasn't any just those two red tears trickling from her eyes. I think I started my period. I crossed a line.

Samba Heat. Jasmine. Peony. I spray it on my wrist skin. My underarms. I want to crawl into the bottle. Live inside pink glass. Water lily. Black Currant.

I can always visit the long ago. I spray on avatar roses, see the white throated woman back in my past. Her name was Cyndi. She let my father's friends kiss her. "All of them are peacocks," she said, "resting it on the ground." Please stay, I thought, don't go away. She leaned against the dresser. The perfume decanter was the prettiest thing in the room. She fingered the cloudy glass of the stopper ball where the scent left was tawny and dried. She touched it behind my ears. "You're a sweet thing." Then she hugged me. "I wish your da would let me take you home." Cyndi's long brown hair felt like feathers, soft and warm. I wanted the stopper ball. Perfume like crushed leaves held a precious sweetness of the tree. More Samba. Perfume makes me invisible. Lilies and mint. Nutmeg and musk. This one is cedar and gardenia. I spray all of them on. I make a mortuary.

"You have to pay for that bottle," the clerk says, stepping out from behind the elevated check-out. He pushes aside the perfume fog. He's tall and Indian, handsome with black hair that looks too silky to be real. People are smaller when the cash register isn't between you and them. But he holds himself like he's the owner. "You pay, then get out." He passes a hand over his rich black hair. Like black ice cream. What flavor would that be? I tell him I don't have money. "You take your dirt. Go." I see my eyes floating in the round mirror above the counter but where is my face?

There I am on TV. Shoplifting Network. They're all from Bangladesh in the delis, working twelve hour shifts, and young dark-eyed guys who I smile at and who always smile (shyly) back. No matter if Indians or Koreans own the store, they get Bangladeshis. They work, they keep on working. Fourteen, sixteen hours. Whatever it is that lies behind them, they keep saying "next," their fingers quick on the register. Starving owls bring fish and frogs into the nest. Now you enter the store, stand out in your red sweats, red hoodie, sneakers brand new from Payless Shoes. You strut like a peacock in full array. Each eye, gold, green, purple. "How about a hand job from this girl for two six-packs of Heineken and a box of fig cookies? How about it, brother?" Now you badger him, wanting a sandwich too. Ham and cheese with oil and onions and a pickle on the side. *Will you bind a wild bull fast with its ropes in the furrows?* The counter boy freezes, the smile still on his lips. I smooth my blond hair. Now a couple sidles in, tall and dreadlocked. In uptown leather pants and claret-colored velvet vests. Ethiopian gazelles. I clutch fig cookies, counting out dimes. The nice-faced boy shakes his head. "No charge." Then he says, "next," and the gazelles step to the counter. Meals in the Ethiopia of long ago—the tongues of flamingoes and the brains of peacocks. Outside on the street the heat presses down, breathes what it wants of us, and blows stale half air at our backs.

Pick up the pace," you say. "Two more avenues to Port Authority. We're going to find a hotel in East Harlem. Get our faces off the street. You're just as guilty as me. Remember that. What are you gawking at?" You stroke your goatee so pointed and black it could be made out of coal. "They find me they find you. Understand?" The heat wants to peel the faces from the canyon of glass, the billboards with the beautiful huge people peering down. "I gotta make a call." You lean against the building, talk on the girl's cell phone.

Port Authority depot swarms. The pretzel sellers are burning dough on the corner, twisting it. You want two with mustard on it. First we have to make money. Through the electronic doors and down the escalator to the bus gates. You walk behind me. There at gate 73 the door from the loading zone opens and a stream of weary people straggle in. In baggy jeans and purple muumuus, in bedroom slippers. The overweight driver, a white-haired guy with a cigarette in his mouth, climbs down from the bus. You approach him. "Want a date?" The driver glances over at me, takes a puff of his cigarette. Nods. He throws down his smoke, re-boards and I follow him. He doesn't sit in the driver's seat, but closes the door and leads me a few seats back. "Sweetheart, make it quick. They're going to be cleaning in here." I take down his zip and reach in and bring him out. I lick my lips because men like that. Like I'm hungry for it. I can inhale the three hundred mile long drive. I think of my favorite red knit sweater dress with a V cut away back. I'm kneeling between an empty can of Vienna sausages and a Burger King Santa Fe Salad. I'm tasting him. It's a smallish thing. He's breathing normally, and then he's panting. Afterwards, he touches my hair. "You look like a nice girl," he says, raising his zip. He has beautiful blue eyes in a flat tire of a face. "Here's an extra twenty. Get away from that thug."

You're on the girl's cell again. You beckon me, a finger wag. You take the money, peel off a five dollar bill. "Go get me two pretzels. Hurry."

The pretzel man. His eyes like burnt dough look out of a long thin face. "Two with mustard," I say. He slips the crinkly paper under each, lifts the mustard bottle and a ribbon of yellow wiggles from its nostril. The brown man fingers the smoke, the miniature world where his hands live. I don't think I'll fetch two pretzels for you. I tuck the paper sack under my arm, pull dough apart and scatter the pieces. Pigeons scuttle around my feet. Pigeons are my favorites. Traipsing this way and that on their red legs. Their feathers muted orange blue gray radiance, the most beautiful things on this earth. "That one," the pretzel man laughs, pointing at the dark grey pigeon with rainbow neck. "He comes everyday. Fat as a cat." The pit of my stomach is caught in gnarl and gristle. I look down the street. I take a bite, lick mustard and watch the big one eat.

I never knew my mother. My father laughed and told me I was hatched. *For she leaves her eggs to the earth itself. And in the dust she keeps them warm.*

When I was three and four my room held one window. The building's air shaft looked in, although sun never did. When cold hunched its shoulder against the glass, pigeons huddled on the ledge. In bitter snow they flew to warm themselves, I watched them fall into the air and then fly up. Others fell, their wings frozen, didn't open. I couldn't see to the bottom of the shaft where pigeons died. I carried my blanket to the window to warm them. I tried to push the glass up but it was nailed shut. Sometimes Cyndi brought me pretzels. In a little box the pretzels rested side by side, not twisted but straight as sticks. We counted them together. "Twenty five," she'd say and her voice sounded like a purr. She would get down on her knees, push aside all her smoky brown hair and bite and tease me. Her lips outlined in dark roses and bruises from all the men kisses.

Once she brought a rubber ball and six-tipped metal things. I put one in my mouth and tried to chew it. Cyndi laughed. "For fucks sake, you're more like a little animal, aren't you?" She took the jack from me. "I'm going to teach you." We sat on the green rug with the rose in the center and bounced the ball. Onesies. Twosies. "Poor little animal you don't even talk." She let me climb into her lap to snuggle there and wrap the warm brown hair through my fingers. "Your da was a Shakespearian actor before he became a pimp and he can't put words in his own child's mouth." After she left I stood at the window. White pigeons roosted on the ledge. I kissed them through the glass. Coo roo. I talked back in their language. Coo roo. Coo roo. The white pigeon with blue rainbow iridescence at his neck told me I was their friend.

I give the pretzel man a dollar tip and just then police cars pull up alongside 42nd Street. An NYPD van stops at the curb and policemen jump out. I search for mustard in the corner of my mouth. Brawny men in blue uniforms rush into the Port Authority. Hands at their belts, guns. Another car squeals up. More blue men. I walk away. You are a peacock roasted and served its own plumage.

I keep walking. Blue Ruin, the leather bar with go-go dancers in mesh thongs, flat beer in a chlorine-scented dark. In the window of a bookstore Barack and Michelle Obama paper dolls and cut outs for sale. Smith's Bar & Grill. If I had money I would go inside. I keep walking toward the light, stop, take another bite. The pretzel is good, but the mustard is better. I tear off more bread. A checkered brown pigeon hurries toward the crumbs. Do you know why a pigeon will eat almost anything? It has only 37 taste buds. A person has 9,000. Cyndi told me that long ago.

I keep on moving toward Broadway, past the theaters with their smoky exteriors. *Phantom of the Opera* and Monty Python's *Spamalot*. Frankie and Johnny's Steakhouse. Two Guardian Angels patrol a corner of the sidewalk and when I pass by one of them winks. A police car careens down Eighth Avenue. I feel the red breath of its siren. It passes through me like a red knife. Terrible is the taste of the forbidden. The girl whose whole body hundreds of flamingo tongues covered.

The dead girl was a bakery tier of cupcakes in fortresses of frosting. Marzipan peaches and strawberries. I'm an order of coffee. Chicory here, that harsh bitter brew made from bark. I'll keep walking. I'll never stop. I picture my history teacher. I think of the tank girls who volunteered for the Battle of Stalingrad, the partisan girls, Zoya and Masha, one hanged by a thin noose and left to slowly strangle, another high from an ash tree, her feet floating out of her shoes. Girls who went to their deaths without batting an eyelash. I think of the girl in the dumpster. Why hadn't I run?

SPUYTEN DUYVIL
Meeting Eyes Bindery
Triton

8TH AVENUE   Stefan Brecht
A DAY AND A NIGHT AT THE BATHS   Michael Rumaker
ACTS OF LEVITATION   Laynie Browne
ALIEN MATTER   Regina Derieva
ANARCHY   Mark Scroggins
APO/CALYPSO   Gordon Osing
APPLES OF THE EARTH   Dina Elenbogen
ARC: CLEAVAGE OF GHOSTS   Noam Mor
THE ARSENIC LOBSTER   Peter Grandbois
AUNTIE VARVARA'S CLIENTS   Stelian Tanase
BALKAN ROULETTE   Drazan Gunjaca
THE BANKS OF HUNGER AND HARDSHIP   J. Hunter Patterson
BLACK LACE   Barbara Henning
BREATHING BOLAÑO   Thilleman & Blevins
BREATHING FREE   (ed.) Vyt Bakaitis
BURIAL SHIP   Nikki Stiller
BUTTERFLIES   Brane Mozetic
*BY THE TIME YOU FINISH THIS BOOK
    YOU MIGHT BE DEAD*   Aaron Zimmerman
CAPTIVITY NARRATIVES   Richard Blevins
CELESTIAL MONSTER   Juana Culhane
CLEOPATRA HAUNTS THE HUDSON   Sarah White
COLUMNS: TRACK 2   Norman Finkelstein
CONSCIOUSNESS SUITE   David Landrey
*THE CONVICTION & SUBSEQUENT
    LIFE OF SAVIOR NECK*   Christian TeBordo

CONVICTION'S NET OF BRANCHES   Michael Heller
THE CORYBANTES   Tod Thilleman
CROSSING BORDERS   Kowit & Silverberg
DAY BOOK OF A VIRTUAL POET   Robert Creeley
THE DESIRE NOTEBOOKS   John High
DETECTIVE SENTENCES   Barbara Henning
DIARY OF A CLONE   Saviana Stanescu
DIFFIDENCE   Jean Harris
DONNA CAMERON   Donna Cameron
DON'T KILL ANYONE, I LOVE YOU   Gojmir Polajnar
DRAY-KHMARA AS A POET   Oxana Asher
EGGHEAD TO UNDERHOOF   Tod Thilleman
THE EVIL QUEEN   Benjamin Perez
EXTREME POSITIONS   Stephen Bett
THE FARCE   Carmen Firan
FISSION AMONG THE FANATICS   Tom Bradley
THE FLAME CHARTS   Paul Oppenheimer
FLYING IN WATER   Barbara Tomash
FORM   Martin Nakell
GESTURE THROUGH TIME   Elizabeth Block
GHOSTS!   Martine Bellen
GIRAFFES IN HIDING   Carol Novack
GOD'S WHISPER   Dennis Barone
GOWANUS CANAL, HANS KNUDSEN   Tod Thilleman
HALF-GIRL   Stephanie Dickinson
HIDDEN DEATH, HIDDEN ESCAPE   Liviu Georgescu
HOUNDSTOOTH   David Wirthlin
IDENTITY   Basil King
IN TIMES OF DANGER   Paul Oppenheimer
INCRETION   Brian Strang
INFINITY SUBSECTIONS   Mark DuCharme

INVERTED CURVATURES   Francis Raven
JACKPOT   Tsipi Keller
THE JAZZER & THE LOITERING LADY   Gordon Osing
KNOWLEDGE   Michael Heller
LADY V.   D.R. Popa
LAST SUPPER OF THE SENSES   Dean Kostos
A LESSER DAY   Andrea Scrima
LET'S TALK ABOUT DEATH   M. Maurice Abitbol
LIGHT HOUSE   Brian Lucas
LIGHT YEARS: MULTIMEDIA IN THE EAST
               VILLAGE, 1960-1966   (ed.) Carol Bergé
LITTLE BOOK OF DAYS   Nona Caspers
LITTLE TALES OF FAMILY & WAR   Martha King
LONG FALL: ESSAYS AND TEXTS   Andrey Gritsman
LUNACIES   Ruxandra Cesereanu
LUST SERIES   Stephanie Dickinson
LYRICAL INTERFERENCE   Norman Finkelstein
MAINE BOOK   Joe Cardarelli (ed. Anselm Hollo)
MANNHATTeN   Sarah Rosenthal
MEDIEVAL OHIO   Richard Blevins
MEMORY'S WAKE   Derek Owens
MERMAID'S PURSE   Laynie Browne
MOBILITY LOUNGE   David Lincoln
THE MOSCOVIAD   Yuri Andrukhovych
MULTIFESTO: A HENRI D'MESCAN READER   Davis Schneiderman
NO PERFECT WORDS   Nava Renek
NO WRONG NOTES   Norman Weinstein
NORTH & SOUTH   Martha King
NOTES OF A NUDE MODEL   Harriet Sohmers Zwerling
OF ALL THE CORNERS TO FORGET   Gian Lombardo
OUR FATHER   M.G. Stephens

OVER THE LIFELINE   Adrian Sangeorzan
PART OF THE DESIGN   Laura E. Wright
PIECES FOR SMALL ORCHESTRA & OTHER FICTIONS   Norman Lock
A PLACE IN THE SUN   Lewis Warsh
THE POET : PENCIL PORTRAITS   Basil King
POLITICAL ECOSYSTEMS   J.P. Harpignies
POWERS: TRACK 3   Norman Finkelstein
PRURIENT ANARCHIC OMNIBUS   j/j Hastain
RETELLING   Tsipi Keller
ROOT-CELLAR TO RIVERINE   Tod Thilleman
THE ROOTS OF HUMAN SEXUALITY   M. Maurice Abitbol
SAIGON AND OTHER POEMS   Jack Walters
A SARDINE ON VACATION   Robert Castle
SAVOIR FEAR   Charles Borkhuis
SECRET OF WHITE   Barbara Tomash
SEDUCTION   Lynda Schor
SEE WHAT YOU THINK   David Rosenberg
SETTLEMENT   Martin Nakell
SEX AND THE SENIOR CITY   M. Maurice Abitbol
SLAUGHTERING THE BUDDHA   Gordon Osing
THE SPARK SINGER   Jade Sylvan
SPIRITLAND   Nava Renek
STRANGE EVOLUTIONARY FLOWERS   Lizbeth Rymland
SUDDENLY TODAY WE CAN DREAM   Rutha Rosen
THE SUDDEN DEATH OF...   Serge Gavronsky
THE TAKEAWAY BIN   Toni Mirosevich
TALKING GOD'S RADIO SHOW   John High
TED'S FAVORITE SKIRT   Lewis Warsh
THINGS THAT NEVER HAPPENED   Gordon Osing
THIS GUY   James Lewelling

THREAD   Vasyl Makhno
THREE MOUTHS   Tod Thilleman
THREE SEA MONSTERS   Tod Thilleman
TRACK   Norman Finkelstein
TRANSITORY   Jane Augustine
TRANSPARENCIES LIFTED FROM NOON   Chris Glomski
TSIM-TSUM   Marc Estrin
VIENNA ØØ   Eugene K. Garber
UNCENSORED SONGS FOR SAM ABRAMS   (ed.) John Roche
WARP SPASM   Basil King
WATCHFULNESS   Peter O'Leary
WALKING AFTER MIDNIGHT   Bill Kushner
WEST OF WEST END   Peter Freund
WHIRLIGIG   Christopher Salerno
WHITE, CHRISTIAN   Christopher Stoddard
WITHIN THE SPACE BETWEEN   Stacy Cartledge
WRECKAGE OF REASON   (ed.) Nava Renek
THE YELLOW HOUSE   Robin Behn
YOU, ME, AND THE INSECTS   Barbara Henning

Made in the USA
Charleston, SC
29 October 2011